THE NEW B

PRESENTS

TOWERS

Karl Fischer

To Jordan,
Thanks for being
so kind and supportive.
I'm wishing you the
best in all
your endeavors

Eraserhead Press
Portland, OR

Best,
Karl Fischer

ERASERHEAD PRESS
P.O. BOX 10065
PORTLAND, OR 97296

WWW.ERASERHEADPRESS.COM

ISBN: 1-62105-198-6

Karl Fischer is a personal friend of mine. We play Mag-ic, hang out, drink. Him, his wife and his pug are among my closest associates in this town. I've had Karl as both a student and a client so I've seen the evolution of his work and it's come quite a long way. He comes across normal, straightlaced and salt-of-the-Earth, a person who has led a life of comfort and simplicity and would rather not have dan-ger or bullshit or risk as part of his situation.

This is not true of Karl. He's a sensitive and deep per-son, a guy who asks a lot of questions and has a strong con-science and a profound sense of duty. Putting together my first NBAS docket, it didn't take much thought to decide this was a guy I wanted in my corner. And he had a manuscript he'd already been working on for the NBAS tThis book has gone through the wringer, and Karl himself has too. The in-ner life of one of the most apparently normal and stable guys you know (granted, I keep the company of a lot of freaks) is sometimes a great surprise, one that unfolds not just for you but for them when they let themselves explore it. This is a brave, difficult and intense book, from a great guy.

This book is really cool. I say that about all these books. Because it's a fucking fact.

— Garrett Cook, Editor

Acknowledgements

This book is half fiction and half love letter. It is dedicated to my wife, my parents, and my sister. None of this would be possible without them.

I love you guys. I owe a great deal to my editor, Garrett Cook, for helping me turn a pile of dream imagery into something coherent and meaningful.

He is a gentleman and a scholar. I would like to thank Spike Marlowe and Michael Allen Rose for convincing me to do the NBAS. And I would like to thank everyone in the Bizarro scene for being so friendly and wonderful and welcoming.

Chapter One

We were Towers and we shattered the sky.

We were three hundred meters tall, anchored to the bedrock on mammoth monopile roots. We were carbide skeletons on which steel and lead and graphene plastic matrices were layered to form oblique, unbreakable skin. But most of all, we were the Gods of Fire and War and Thermonuclear Destruction. When we unleashed Atomic Hounds upon the night's void, every kingdom shuddered and every mortal knew why we were built.

We were Towers.

But we had one weakness: those that lived inside us.

They thought I couldn't feel them walking in the corridors of my marrow and the ventricles of my heart. The human germs crawling and feeding and fucking—sometimes fixing and reloading—but always, always scratching. They caused me to look inward. They did nothing but distract me from the fight.

I was human once, and I remember that it was miserable. Prejudice, anxiety, want—the hallmarks of my short existence. I lived without certainty. But there was certainty in steel. There was certainty in the exhaust of a newly launched missile and the white, celestial explosion that its terminus brought. There was certainty in Quatra.

The time I spent being human was good for only one purpose—to meet Quatra, the singular cog that would mesh with my own.

Alone, we were overwhelmed by the lizard gestalt of our

brains. Brought together, we made of ourselves a functional mechanism. We had a use for all our meltwater emotions. Death, however, reminded us that love did not exist in its stygian paradise. Death could walk, and it arose from the ocean to make war upon the last human cities. In those dying days of civilization, the Towers were built to defend what remained.

So long ago.

Requisition called for people to operate the Towers and we volunteered. Shed the flesh, fight for a thousand years, and in return, be admitted unto the Afterlife. What was a millennium compared to an eternity with Quatra? To be without separation, without sorrow or fear, I would pay any price.

I counted down the days.

A thousand years gone.

But these humans. These viral dwellers. I could feel them inside me, as they were in every Tower, and the sensation repelled certainty. What were they doing to me? I fought with everything I had. What more could they want?

It was my rest period of Day 365,241, my last day of service. I dreamt that Quatra and I were parasites in our own skin, and we were ravenous. We cannibalized muscles of polymer and concrete and went deep into the organ meat of our power plants. We were vermin crawling in cavernous spaces that were wet with blood, yet smelled of dust. Our real bodies, the spires, were dead. The planet was a necropolis and our enemies loomed overhead, breathing hellfire and pulsing clouds of devastation. We could do nothing but weep at the basework of our titanic hearts. We couldn't even hold each other because we didn't know how.

Then I woke up screaming.

Towers don't scream. But I did. Every organ in my body

had a voice. Every organ was trying to expunge something, a pain so deep it went down into the individual cells. Where was Quatra? Where were my missiles?

I could no longer see the radioactive landscape, the churning waters from which Death emerged, not even the dirt to which I was anchored. I saw nothing except ghostly green phantasms amidst a sea of black. And I heard a tiny voice calling my name, followed by an abrupt silence.

"Open your eyes, please."

My body was soft. I felt tiny drums of taut flesh vibrating at the barrage of sound waves.

"Open your eyes, Alti. That is your name, yes?"

I opened my eyes, my new eyes, and I felt like dying all over again.

"Quatra." I said it like a prayer, though I barely comprehended the meat which flapped the name into existence. "Please."

"Just relax. You've got bigger problems now."

"Afterlife?" I baked under the oppressive lights, sweated, squirmed. "Is this the Afterlife?"

"Goodness no." The voice—the human germ that lorded over me—rumbled like a distant takeoff. "You've been reincarnated as a human. You're just like everybody else now."

"I don't understand. I served. I fought. A millennium—"

"Not quite a millennium. A few hours short."

I couldn't process his words—it had to be a nightmare. "Quatra?"

"I don't know what a 'quatra' is. Would you like a sedative? It will help you sleep while we finish calibrating you."

"This isn't the way. I've done my duty. I'm supposed to be in heaven."

9

"Don't be so pathetic." The human's body was almost fluid it was so moist, an alien biomachine, but the sadism in its voice—that reek of low individuality—frightened me even more. "You're not going anywhere. The Tower is our home and we need every person available to ensure the continued survival of our race. You think we can afford to have people lying around in stasis? We call that dereliction of duty. Why should some go to heaven while the rest of us are left to suffer? No, my friend, we will all live and fight and die together."

Something wet was spreading on my flesh. Saltwater leapt from my eyes and ran down my face. I was crying. I could not contain myself. I cried so hard that I ruined my voice.

"We need you, Alti," the doctor said, almost tenderly. "Now more than ever."

At some point I fell asleep again. I dreamt of Quatra, but not as the fiery war machine I knew. The vision was almost too much to bear. Quatra had also been reborn into a human body: two sets of frail limb attached to a fleshy middle. Old memories—human memories—surfaced as I discovered things like gender and height and hair color. Quatra was a woman once more.

"Wake up, Quatra," said a doctor, perhaps even the same doctor that had awakened me. "Only a few hours left, but we couldn't lose you just yet. You are needed in the Tower."

"I am the Tower," said Quatra, her voice so small and so weak. "I should be dead."

"Nonsense. You are very much alive."

"Afterlife," she said, even weaker, on the verge of tears. "It wasn't my fault. Something forced me out of my body."

"Don't worry, my dear, we gave you a new body. As I said, we cannot afford to send you to the Afterlife. I realize this may be inconvenient and perhaps a little unpleasant, but there is still a great deal of work to be done."

"A thousand years. Ten lifetimes of work."

"There's no need to be dramatic. We need you now more than ever, Quatra."

"What about Alti? I want to see Alti."

"There's no such thing as an 'alti.' Let's get you cleaned up and ready for the work floor. Tomorrow you start contributing to society."

Quatra finally broke down, her face rearranging itself into a mess of scrunched lines and fat, leaking fluids. It was more than my stupid heart could take.

Please, Quatra.

Please, I'm still here. I'm still on Earth.

I would never leave you.

Quatra, my love, please don't cry.

She wept bitterly and the disgusting human germ watched her as I pounded on the walls of Sleep. I yelled her name. I yelled for the doctor to stop watching. I squeezed every muscle, willing ordnance to erupt from my body and destroy my enemies. Nothing worked. Defeated, I simply wept with her.

"I'll find you," I said, curling around my horrible new limbs. "I promise."

I woke to a black and featureless coffin. Its barriers formed a cube, barely large enough for even my diminutive body. I realized that it was a room, an enclosed habitation space, thousands of which once existed inside me. Now I was living in one. I was a human in a Tower.

Chapter Two

Arm-in-arm, we ran through the city. Troglodytes beneath a ceiling of thunderheads. Lost in the rain somewhere, we finally made it to a coffeehouse and bludgeoned our brains with caffeine until neither of us could stop laughing. Every detail of her face, every pore and follicle, looked like poetry. I knew even less about poetry than I did about love, but that was the moment I knew for certain.

She swept me up in her gaze and told me a secret that night. A whispered entreaty.

I told her I wanted to sink to the bottom of the ocean with her.

She held me close as we began to drift. "I used to have a lot of jumping dreams. At least once a week. I'd be walking around, maybe running from something or someone, only to realize that I didn't have to stay on the ground like an idiot. I could just push off with my feet and soar through the air. It was more than liberating—it was profound. It was like I'd been untethered from something and could finally be free."

And then she looked kind of embarrassed, but said it anyway. "That's the way I feel with you, Alti. I love you."

I smiled so hard I thought I would break.

I said the same. And I said even more. And I meant it all.

We kissed until we forgot who had which body.

But inside my head, far from all the other lights, something unbidden climbed to the surface of my mind. Something old and full of terror.

The terror arose and it asked me quietly, "What if?"

At first it was only a little.

For years it was only a little.

But in good time, my head began to echo with the sound of the terror's voice and with the volume of its questioning.

What if I was a liar?

What if I didn't mean it?

What if I secretly resented the woman I held in my arms?

What if just threw it all away?

What if?

"You've got to think about it," said the terror in all its somber gravity. "Because you're going to look pretty fucking stupid when it all comes crashing down."

And then one day it wasn't a question, it was a thought. An imperative. A desperate, raving voice that wanted to split my teeth and pour out like vomit.

"I'm worried I don't love you anymore, Quatra." It was an explosion and a confession and it killed me as soon as I said it.

She hardly blinked, but her astral eyes went dark and her jaw began to quiver. "You can't do that to me."

Why would I think it if I didn't mean it? Why would I want to do that?

I didn't. And I knew it wasn't true. No matter how horrible I felt, I knew it wasn't true.

"It's not real, Quatra, it's not real. I would never. Oh, sweetheart. Baby, please, there's something wrong with me. There's something horrible inside telling me that I don't love you, telling me to get out, but it's all a lie. I can feel it in my heart."

I sought to prove it, but there was no amount of evidence that would soothe the panic. In fact, the more evidence I gathered, the more frightened I became. I wanted my heart to break, to feel the orchestral swell in my chest that would drive me to sorrow and tender affection, and sometimes I got my wish, but sometimes I got the hollowness. My heart could pound so hard I'd feel it in my fingertips, and then it would disappear altogether, leaving me in a vacuum where I felt neither the pangs of love nor even the panic that I was about to lose everything.

"I could just kill myself," I offered one night, maybe somewhat joking, but feeling all the same that death would be a relief.

Quatra didn't find it funny.

She threw me from the bed midsentence. Mid-apology. My head barely hit the floor when she came scrambling after me and landed on my chest. The air was pounded from my lungs. I saw a bright flash of early morning light before her hand made contact with my cheek. Each strike put me deeper and deeper below the waves. The pain was miraculous— neither in my head nor in my heart, but right where it was supposed to be. Would that I could have laid there and been slapped forever.

"I'm never going to stop loving you," said Quatra, hand cradling my raw cheek, her voice like an iron ingot. "I don't want you to be sorry. I don't want you to go away. I want you to fight. If I thought that what we have was possible and that it could be lost for no reason at all, it would destroy me. I can't allow it. And you can't either."

In the white space between my ears, she was all violence and color. I couldn't bear the sight of her, but I didn't dare look away. The pure morning light that streamed over her face was suddenly eclipsed as Death itself emerged from the ocean.

There came the rumble and the first of many sirens as the blocks mobilized and the shelters cranked open. Death scuttled from the waves, setting off hundreds of tremors that

I felt in my groin. I could see its antennae arching through the air like suspension cables to another planet. Imagine snipping one off and watching it fall from the sky. To think that I could see only its delicate antennae and not the size of its claws, the segmented arch of its legs, or the juggernaut horror of its bulletproof body. It was all down there, just out of sight beneath the window sill, and there on top of me was my Quatra, waiting for my answer.

We might have had only minutes, for there was no telling where the beast would start its assault or which bombs would go astray. But we didn't move an inch. She sat astride me, tear-streaked, enraged, and in love.

"Sweetie," I said, one finger roving up to her cheek and wiping away a tear, "I have an idea."

Chapter Three

Those who dwelt in the Tower referred to themselves as Oysters. It seemed nonsensical, until I realized they were also confined to an armored shell where life had no purpose except to survive. They kept me sedated for the first few days to make sure I wouldn't kill myself. If only it were that simple. Somewhere in the wide and desolate world, Quatra was trapped inside the body of her own Tower, and if I was going to find her, I would have to do as the Oyster did and survive at all costs.

Adapting to my new body took the greatest amount of care and compromise. I had a drive to keep it clean, yet doing so forced me to contemplate the failure it represented. To that end, the mirror was my enemy. Quatra had been my reflection, and in Quatra I had seen our future in the Afterlife. The silver glass showed me soft, weak, needy, ash-colored human limbs and thorax, erupting with keratin, always molting. This new present mocked the future I had been promised.

When I was finally allowed to join the workforce, I expected the very worst. Everything in the Tower was about work. Every Oyster had a quota and the quota was meant to be broken, because that was how the war would be won. Haul the warheads. Prep the launch bays. Maintain the circuitry. Inspect the motors. Clean the filters. Replace broken parts. Repurpose the dead. Birth the living. Repeat until victory. It was not unlike being a Tower. The job they gave me was "record keeping."

Tell the Record about the Infirmary that day: Coldness.
Vitae. Confusion.

Tell the Record about Manufacturing that day: Noise.
Excitement. Efficiency.

Tell the Record about the Atrium that day: Crowds.
Pheromones. Secrets.

It was all just a matter of applying the right pictograms—
narration was undesirable. There were thousands of
pictograms for all manner of idiom and situation. There were
thousands of Oysters to follow. It didn't seem to matter what
I did or didn't record as long as I recorded something. It
might have been funny if it weren't so nauseatingly tedious.
It brought back memories of my first human job.

I made frequent visits to the doctors so that they could
take my vitals and perform numerous tests on me. They said
I was unstable, that I had to be closely monitored.

"You have a very important task to undertake, Alti," one
of the interchangeable doctors would say. "You are very
special. We cannot risk losing you."

Beyond the doctors and the administrator that I reported
to, I rarely indulged in conversation. As a newcomer with
the least interesting job, I was almost universally ignored.
Almost. There were those stared at me for too long.

Of the outside world, the Oysters seemed to know very
little. The Earth was devoid of humanity except for the
Towers, those hermetically sealed bastions. An Oyster woke
with the alarms, which told them that the sun had risen.
There was no access to the sky, only principled certainty that
celestial bodies functioned as they always had. I wondered if
each Tower held the same ruthlessly efficient and endlessly
recycled biosphere.

The missiles were finite, and once gone, would be gone
forever. I had never considered that the missiles could run

out, that no others were being produced. Did our enemy's numbers dwindle as well? Without even knowing what they were or why they hated us, no one could fathom the answer.

Eating was unnecessary and so there were no official meal times, which meant no respite from work. Our dripping air supply was heavy with planktonic creatures—simple organisms that had no purpose in life but to feed off our waste and be ingested in turn. My lungs strained them from the air constantly. Yet my mouth was still a mouth and a market existed to accommodate that orifice. Nothing was grown in the Tower except for tangerines, the last fruit on Earth. They grew deep beneath the living quarters in a domed forest where only ancient Oysters worked.

To bite them, to feel the flood of juice, tart acid burning delicate receptors, was a joy. I was powerless to resist the tangerines and took every opportunity to stand in line for one. The window of opportunity was always short. Some Oysters willingly suffered the punishments of Absenteeism in order to eat their fill.

Things began to improve for me when I discovered that, while no warmachine, my body could be customized—something that a Tower could not do. Under my skin were trillions of chromatophores, providing a range of visual expression that went far beyond the flailing, undulating, smacking discourse of my feeding parts. Though I did not like the quick and insubstantial nature of my humanity, I fell in love with its colors.

Oysters had to love each other to survive, or so went the theory. When the work was done, communion was held in the Atrium. An hour of fornication. The noises disgusted me—all that squelching and mewling. But worse yet, my body reacted to their pheromones regardless. I hid from prowlers—the lonely ones—and cloistered myself in the highest levels of the Tower, a winding spiral where only cold armor and support beams resided. They would not have me.

In Sleep, Oysters could be together, without distinction or distraction, without divide of any kind. But I did not want their company in my dreams. I craved only one life force. I sought out Quatra. And sometimes, if I was lucky, I could see her coming for me over the blasted landscape of my imagination. We ran to each other. Some night, perhaps, we would touch.

Chapter Four

The sounds of coitus tied me in knots, each loop drawing my stomach tighter and tighter. I could feel mucosa between my legs, the weeping, aching, throbbing flesh that was too stupid to obey my revulsion. A pulsing red light drove me feral. All I could think about was getting to my cell and the lean comfort of my blankets.

They were out there, looking for me. I made it to the door of my cell, but when the footsteps did not fade away, I knew that I would only be trapping myself within four walls.

"Enough foreplay," came the braying, buzzing, insect swarm of a voice. "You're one of us now. You've been hiding for too long—find out what it means to be part of a community. Don't make me beg."

I climbed upward, following the nautilus steps of the Tower's vast inner stairwell. My breathing was loud enough for the horde to pursue. I told my angry, panicked mind that it was okay to run from this enemy. I tried like hell not to think of Quatra.

"I can smell you leaking. I can taste you on the air. You're not getting away this time."

The comingled scent of their ravenous appetites tore my fight or flight response apart. I fled the stairs and stumbled through a darkened, unused hallway. Dust filled my lungs. I was so tired and weak. I found a collapsed alcove, little more than a crack in the wall, and sank into its recess. There I hunched and waited, bile rising in my throat, dread overwhelming. They encircled my hiding spot, their body heat turning it into a furnace. I squirmed and blackened as they grew new horns in anticipation.

"Come out of there," said the horde's leader, his fingers like questing tentacles as they hovered just below my lips. "We can be gentle."

I bit his finger. They were not gentle.

I was dragged screaming and pressed into the floor. I was luminescent, my skin throwing their horrid faces into candlelit relief. I opened my mouth to expel the panic and they plugged it. I howled around their flesh and it drove them onward. My legs were forced apart, knees screaming as they forced me open and widened me. I was being ripped apart, shooting pains radiating from my gut, a pressure like my innards wanted to swell out of my throat.

"There's no meat like fresh meat," said the horde. "He's about ready to pop."

Something soft encircled my genitals. I instantly thought of being with Quatra, connected with her at our softest points. What was agony to a Tower? Nothing except a little patience. A Tower's memories could not be harmed. But I was no longer a Tower. They pumped the life from me, forced it out like pus from a wound. They penetrated me to the core. And when it was all over, they stole my memories, turning the only beauty of my human life into something terrible.

Sight failed me—there was little to see but the floor and the press of bodies—and I thought, long and loud, "I hope that I die soon."

They departed one be one, leaving me a little colder each time.

I lay there for some time, ooze pouring from every orifice. I had no control over the shaking of my muscles. I was hollow inside.

The alarms signaled the end of communion and I dragged myself back to my cell, ignoring the other Oysters who were returning to theirs. The blankets were cool and neutral. The darkness was good because it kept me from having to see my flesh.

I didn't want to think about Quatra. Instead, I became three hundred meters tall again. I beheld a fertile plain, a world denied to me. Grasses waved like billions of tiny hands, their applause both soft and overwhelming.

I strode on gargant feet and trod through the ages. My heart quietly died.

When I finally collapsed, I watched the curve of the Earth. I left a crater large enough to name, yet it was just a speck on the prairie's body. All was quiet. My corpse began to rot, the decay gradually accelerating as I looked on.

When I was all the way dead, I was allowed to resurrect as a giant skeleton with bloody tangerines for guts and a skull filled with spores that wafted gently out all my cracks and cavities. I roved the lush, verdant world of my ancestors and dipped my skeletal head into pools of water. There was nothing better than cool, clear water.

"You are stuck in the comforts of the past," said a voice. "Where you are needed is the pain of the future."

My naked bones stood at attention. Water dripped from my eye sockets and tickled my nasal cavity.

A creature appeared to me. It had no arms, no legs, seemingly no head, but a preponderance of torso and neck meat. Its body formed a column—a tower—bald flesh rooted to the dirt. Flares and bristles and nematocysts bubbled on its skin, creating patterns, language, poetry, weapons.

"Is it really death that you crave?"

I looked at my claws, unable to imagine holding anyone with them. Unable to imagine intimacy. What else could I be good for? I could not love and I could not be loved.

"That's nonsense. I'm never going to stop loving you, Alti."

I scrutinized the column of flesh.

"I'm never going to stop loving you. So you can't give up."

The water that ran from my eye sockets became salty. New patches of flesh grew on my bony dome while the tangerines rotted, dropping one by one from my ribcage.

"I don't want to die, Quatra. I want to be with you."

"Then you must suffer," she said, towering above me as I shrank. "And you must build yourself back up."

My heartbeat woke me ahead of the alarm. I couldn't get enough air. I threw the blanket off with hands that were now heavy, almost metallic. The digits had fused into human pincers, the chitinous texture running up past my wrists.

I needed a tangerine.

Chapter Five

We have built for you, among the stars, a place where all peoples and all nations can be reconciled. Let none say that the world comes to an end, for the faithful servant shall receive life eternal. In this we are whole. In this we are equal. The Earth rejects you, but Heaven belongs to those who welcome it.

Into such bullhorn proclamations we stepped, queueing up with other scared, exhausted, and desperate people. The PA system crackled, the voice on the other end sounding much aggrieved. The shoreline heaved with red and foamy waves. Wreckage studded the bay as though a swamp full of bones. The last of the morning mist could be seen hovering in the undemolished portions of the waterfront district. At a time when commuters should have been most plentiful, the streets were wracked with silence.

The Beast is in the tide and God lays dormant underground. God hates that which you are, but the Hands do not. The Hands make the Sun to shine, the grass to grow, the fruit to pluck. All wealth comes from labor. So let us labor, friends, and let us ascend as the tree ascends. Return not to the Earth. Let us tower above the weeds and the ruins. Let us dwell eternal in a paradise of our own making.

Quatra pressed her head to my shoulder, telling me she was still at my side. It was hard to remember why sometimes. My head would randomly scream at me, issuing low bass notes of fear that would vibrate in my guts. But I had to remember that it was only fear. It was only an emotion and it needn't carry any weight. A world of veridicality existed beyond my body, and I had to remember it. I would not be a slave to impulse.

"We should just go home, Alti."

I frowned at the back of her head. "Are you really doing this now?"

She didn't look at me. "A thousand years is a long time."

"They're going to turn us into buildings. Our whole perception of time will be altered."

"Assuming they'll accept us both for the position. Assuming there are any positions left."

"Alright, fine. We'll go home then. And tomorrow or the next day or the day after that, we'll die. Would you prefer that?"

She didn't answer right away. "It seems like a bunch of bullshit—the world ending just when I started to like it."

I angled her head so that our eyes could meet. "There's nothing I wouldn't do for you."

She smiled sadly.

I looked out at the crimson water and the silver stripe reflection of the massive defense tower that would soon be complete. The river that once divided the city was choked with collapsed bridges. Abandoned high-rises bore tooth marks.

"If you want us to be humans then we can be humans," I said. "We'll sign up as laborers and we'll live in the Tower until we can't work anymore and they turn us into mulch."

"Spend the rest of my life in a tin can? Fuck that."

"Exactly! You told me to fight, so that's what we're doing. I don't care how many years it takes because we'll be together in the end. Isn't that what matters?"

She looked doubtful a moment and it put talons in my heart.

The ocean rippled, the surface breaking gently. A wave was swelling higher and higher.

"If it makes you happy," she said, leaning into me, "and it keeps you from being afraid, then I'll do it."

"You seemed unsure for a moment there." I tried to cut myself off, stop the anxiety before it could start, but it was already brewing. "A thousand years is a long time, but the Afterlife will be even longer."

Quatra kissed the pulse at my throat. "It's not me that I'm worried about, darling."

"What are you saying?"

"I'm saying that if you asked me to, I would become a sentient defense tower and throw nukes at sea monsters, which is what we plan to do. And if you asked me to, I would leave right now, take you home, and fuck your brains out until our apartment collapsed on top of us. I would do either one. I just want to be sure that you would too."

My stomach dropped into my legs. I almost couldn't stand how her eyes reflected my stupid little face back at me. I wanted to throw up.

She kissed me again, undeterred. "I know you're in there, Alti."

"I wish I knew that."

She sighed and put my arm around her shoulder. "I've no doubt there will be operator positions available. No one in their right mind wants to spend the next thousand years dealing with the apocalypse."

I wondered if the guy on the loudspeaker had always been employed to shout at people.

The bay inverted, a shimmering dome rising high into the air. The dome ruptured and the water parted in bloody chops, bearing a tangled kelp forest of jaws and yellow scales, like paper snakes erupting from a can. They twisted upward as one lernaean entity, a splendid nightmare, the sky, the clouds, and the sea all forgotten. Moments later the bay exploded, and then kept on exploding as artillery from every rooftop of the city lobbed round after round at the water. The monster, however, continued its inexorable progress.

Will there be any supplication from Leviathan? Will it speak to you in soft words?

Will it make with you a covenant? Will it serve you till the end of days?

What bullet can pierce its skin? What ordnance can sear its hide?

Buildings were knocked sideways while others caved in at sudden velocity. The monster had projectiles of its own. I put as much of myself around Quatra as I could, praying desperately to the god of my ancestors that it would be enough to save her.

There can be no oblivion in the face of Leviathan. There can be no victory against it.

When it rises from the waves, the mighty are terrified. They go without courage.

Behold Leviathan. None are made to rival it.

The calamity was more than deafening. It silenced us like a church. The crowds melted away as water and sewage crawled up the street. The shockwaves made my teeth rattle. The asphalt danced beneath our feet.

Leviathan is subject to no one. It regards all proud things.

So it is not pride that stands against it. It is not might that trumps wickedness.

It is the wreckage of our hearts that makes a Tower against Leviathan.

Our hands clasped tight, we ran to the front of the line where the soldiers and the PA guy and an admin with a clipboard all stood like statues. They watched us run as if they had been waiting for us all along. The sky caught fire and the monster writhed in furious agony.

It is the sum of our tragedy that will defend us from evil.

We lift ourselves to Heaven. And Leviathan follows not.

We leave the Earth unto Leviathan. And there it shall remain.

Chapter Six

I spent more and more time haunting the entrance to the tangerine orchard. Its vestibule had a sharpness to it that was distinct from the rest of the Tower's curvaceous, drippy architecture, which comforted me somehow. It was like stepping into the outside world, or perhaps, like stepping backward into a time when there was an outside world. Between bites of tangerine, I could almost swear I was not spread along a timeline of centuries, but contained in the exhalations of my lungs and the beating of my human heart.

I could no longer remember being patient as steel. I was a thousand years younger.

I remembered a fateful moment, long ago, in which I scrutinized the intravenous feeding pod that would sustain my frail human body until my consciousness could be transferred into something grander. There was a terrible reluctance, but also sadness.

"Come along, Operator," the administrator had said to me, gesturing at my destiny. "You've a deep sleep ahead and all the horrors of Nod to go with it."

Had that reluctance ever left me? Or had it become subsumed into my being?

Keeping records became infinitely more difficult with pincers. A moment's distraction, a tensing of the muscles, and I would puncture my data pad. I was breaking them at a prodigious rate. It didn't help that the other Oysters were taking unwanted interest in my transformation.

And, of course, there were the times when certain faces

looked a little too familiar. Seeing them would cause me to retch, but I could not allow myself to panic until I was back in my cell. I always felt as though I had committed a grave betrayal. Each panic attack felt like a day's worth of work.

Most nights, I walked across a continent of sand, the ocean roaring on either side of it. The continent wrapped around the entire planet and formed a Mobius strip. Quatra and I were on opposite coordinates, continuously repulsed, unable to change direction, unable to meet. There were no Towers, only massive bivalves that glinted of metal. When the tide rolled in, it brought many races of crustacean to the beach. They raised their claws in unison and beat out a steady, pulsing rhythm.

The waves parted, the water bubbling red, the air filling with the stink of putrefaction. The ocean became a vitreous, frothing hallway unto a benthic kingdom, and out in the abyssal plain, something stirred. Though it was so far away, I could clearly see its radiant gaze.

One night, I went to the orchard and waited there until morning, not sleeping a minute. When the arborists arrived, they stopped in their tracks and looked at me with contempt.

"Please," I said, propped against the wall, nostrils flaring at the scent of fresh dirt on the other side. "Just one more."

They watched me watching them.

"There's something terrible inside me. I just want to feel better."

Each of them had a face like a gnarled tree root. One of them opened the doors and went inside. I tried to follow him but the others blocked my way. Moments later, the Oyster returned with a glistening orange gem, the ripest tangerine I'd ever seen. My mouth watered and my throat quivered. I wanted to cry with relief.

They allowed me to eat in peace. I didn't resist when

their arms, thick and strong as tree branches, hoisted me up and took me straight to the doctor's. Everyone stared at me along the way, and for a fleeting moment, it looked like one in the crowd had pincers too.

The doctor's office was a pod of unknown instrumentality and grayish walls. Waiting behind a tidy desk was the same creature who first interrupted my tour of duty and brought me kicking and screaming into the Tower's inner world—I hadn't seen him since. I could hardly tell one Oyster from another, but I knew his scent.

I took a seat and the doctor immediately took liberties with my flesh, patting it and poking it with his slimy hands.

"Alti, you infant, why have you done this?" He tapped at my chitin and made sucking noises with his tongue and teeth. "Why would you develop these pincers? You cannot work with crab claws. You won't be able to keep accurate records. This will not do, Alti. We need you now more than ever."

I tried to argue with the doctor. I had so many things to tell him, so many questions unanswered, but I couldn't focus long enough on any particular one. Instead, I got bogged down with details and just started complaining about the workload. Why was it important that I be efficient anyway? I was not a real Oyster. I shouldn't be held to the same standard. Why did they even need me?

"Utter nonsense. You are 100% Oyster."

I gestured at my claws. Could he explain those?

"We know everything about your body, its tolerances, its genetics, its place in the evolutionary ladder, and so forth. Obviously, there's been some kind of catastrophic mutation."

Had I been tampered with? Was someone trying to sabotage me?

"Your consciousness was transferred directly into a non-sensate and metabolically locked Oyster clone,

31

which became active upon receiving your neural engine. Impossible to sabotage. What you are experiencing is a genetic malfunction, and it can be corrected."

Sadness tore my chest open. The tears came unbidden. Wracked with sobs, I told the doctor what the demons had done to me and that I was terrified it would happen again. I was so afraid. All the time I was afraid. I just wanted to feel better again.

The doctor merely frowned. "Those who accosted you did what was in their nature to do. If you had just accepted your place in this community, it wouldn't have happened that way. Even now, you remain aloof and go begging for tangerines. There's nothing for it."

I begged him to be kind.

"You have chosen to pine for a love that does not exist. You seek happiness from others and it will destroy you. Surely you understand that? Your capabilities are crucial and must not be jeopardized."

What fucking capabilities? What was he talking about?

"There's no need to get hostile. You want to see Quatra again?"

My tears were staunched and my sobbing reduced to a shudder.

"You want to see Quatra again, yes?"

"You said you didn't know who she was." My voice crawled out of my throat and died.

The doctor took me from my seat and brought me to the operating room that adjoined his office. The antiseptic stench, the white sterility—it was like waking up all over again. There were bright lights and black machinery and a host of Oysters with their backs turned, all clustered around something.

"I believe this is the young woman in question," said the

doctor, gesturing at the group. "Ladies? Alti is here to see you."

They turned around one by one.

They were all Quatra. They were all my Quatra, my cog, my counterpart. But they were broken. They had eyes missing and teeth smashed in and bloody, gaping wounds—and it was my fault. Their skin was gangrenous and their hands were cubes of flesh. The more I stared, the more it seemed they bore no resemblance, for their bodies were made from the worst geometry, the meanest intersections of memory and form. And yet their smell. They smelled of Quatra. They were all my love and my life and I didn't recognize a single one of them.

The doctor clapped me on that back. "You see? Alive and well. And in such variety."

What had they done?

"All your memories were kept on a ten thousand year hard drive. We scoured it for any mention of 'Quatra' and implemented what we saw. We thought this might help you adjust."

The Quatras were changing before my eyes, some becoming obese, some emaciated, others mutating beyond any facsimile. Flesh folded on flesh, warping into carbuncles and pearls of gristle. They wept into their breasts and tore at their clothes. They leaked effluvium and begged me to fuck them. And it was all my fault. Every interpretation and movement and violent quaking of the flesh.

"This is what you fought for, Alti. These are your memories. This is what she means to you. Embrace her. Be happy. Love your Quatra and become one with us."

I looked at the doctor.

"Don't you see? We need you here. We can't afford to lose you."

I took the doctor's round little face in my pincers. His lips flapped impotently at me.

"You lied to me," I said. "You've lied to me from the very beginning."

"We're trying to protect you." The doctor looked apprehensive—no longer in control. "What are you thinking?"

I grabbed at his stomach and squeezed. There came a slick and heavy squelching. The doctor shuddered, coughing up liquid as he slumped against me. I reached for his neck and took hold of the delicate vertebrae. An audible pop signaled the end of spinal unity.

The Quatras wailed.

The doctor toppled to the floor, his navel ripped open and festooned with colorful organ meats. The muscles of his body had gone slack. He looked like a vivisected frog. His distended mouth howled out a final, anguished moment. If not already dead, he soon was under the trampling feet of his creations—such was their fervor to stampede me into submission.

I fled the operating room, trailing lacerations and spatters of blood. I vaulted down the spiraling stairs, blind with terror, but unwilling to lose myself until I was somewhere dark. And when I found a spot at last, away from the pounding of machinery and footsteps, I clutched my heart and held onto my brain for dear life.

Chapter Seven

I sat on my haunches, weeping bitter tears, and gasped over and over again. My lungs couldn't get enough air. I could feel every part of me panicking at once. My limbs shook so hard they buzzed. My brain was unable to do anything except bury itself under frenzied recursion.

If you loved Quatra, you wouldn't feel this way.

But I do love Quatra. That's why I feel so bad.

Then go back to her and be happy.

I can't. I'm afraid.

If you loved Quatra, you wouldn't feel this way...

What, after all, did I know about love outside of this illusion, deception, or victim that was named Quatra? What could she know of an entity named Alti? The Alti that had warred for a thousand years was a creature without hunger or panic or self-pity. The Alti that gripped itself and pleaded with his own brain for respite shared only a name with that former life.

I hid myself away, not moving, not working, just waiting for misery to stop and for my heart to harden. I don't know how long I remained that way.

In time, however, I caught myself slinking toward the orchard to feed my obsession for sweetness. I just needed to feel better. Even for a moment. The rush of citrus feelings, the quiet assurance that everything would be okay. Just a little more and I would make it.

I approached the orchard expecting an ambush.

And there was an ambush, but it had not been for me.

Standing just before the doors, several Oysters were clustered around another humanoid lying on the ground. The victim was slight of build, barely a shadow on the floor, and as I stepped into the light of the vestibule, I heard a voice that nearly dropped me to my knees.

"Please," said the voice of Quatra. "Please don't."

Now that I could see them, the Oysters were all too familiar. They were the ones who had chased me up the stairs and into a dead end. They had cored me out and filled me up with fear. They had despoiled my memories and now they were here to finish the job.

There were four of them. They didn't notice until I was very close.

Their leader saw me first and stepped from the group, touting his nakedness like a club. I could see that he recognized me. His lips curled into a sneer. One by one they shifted their attention away from the person on the floor, sizing me up as I flexed one claw and then the other.

"Go back to your room," said the leader, ambling forward. "Communion hour is almost over. We'll find you tomorrow."

I allowed him to come to me. I feared him with every ounce my being, but I could see Quatra in the corner of my eye, and I feared for her even more.

"Go," the leader commanded. "Tomorrow."

I caught a whiff of his breath, still fresh with tangerines. "There'll be no tomorrow."

"Is that so?" His cock waved at my belly. "Alright then. I'll make time for you."

He tried to use his size against me. He was an onslaught of fine musculature, but none of that mattered when he chose to pin my throat and not my arms. We fell to the ground, a sprawling tackle that disoriented me. But I managed to get one pincer between his legs.

He seized up when the two halves met, cutting through all those sensitive cords and tissues. I could feel his screams against my forehead. I twisted my claw and dug in for the rest of the roots as well as the artery. He bled out and I rolled him off as soon as the connection was severed. His companions did nothing to help him—they were either too stunned or too stupid. We locked eyes as blood trickled off my claw tips, tingling in the irritated crevices of my cracked skin.

"Wrong weapon."

I brandished the mangled organ like a knife and threw it at them. It ricocheted off someone's torso and rolled out of sight.

"Try again."

Now they were spurred to action.

Had they always been so large and mean and jagged looking? They transformed right before my eyes, bones to blades, fists that morphed into hooks and saws and hammer drills—mechanical insect machinery that leaked bilious fluid. They grew a meter each. They expelled their heat and it made my vision swim.

The mass of them, their overwhelming size, nearly pulled me to my knees. The urge to lie down turned my stance to jelly.

But there she was, my Quatra, splayed out on the ground like a corpse.

"Are you on Earth?" she asked. "Are you in Heaven?"

"Here," I said, breathing deep. "I'm right here."

"Then which is Leviathan? Them?"

The demons loomed overhead.

"Or you?"

They were the wave and I the rock. They ran aground on my claws. I forced them to react, and with every step back,

I took something of theirs. Sweat dripped and blood ran hot. I snatched at their windpipes, severed their wrists, and cut holes in their bellies. They emptied themselves into piles of offal, falling all around me, their malice vanishing as smoke. By the time I could breathe, they had been carved to pieces.

I staggered from the ruin of their corpses and made my way to the figure on the ground. Trembling, I took the delicate face into my weaponized hands. Its skin fell away at my touch. Quatra fell away, turned to dust. What remained was an alien face, swaddled in the remnants of my woman.

Its physiology was undeniably masculine, yet something about him indicated that "he" was inherently genderless. The eyes were blank marble—looking into them was like reading an unintelligible pictogram. I continued to cradle it, longing for Quatra to return. Eventually, the creature stirred.

"Hello, Alti," it said.

I dropped its head onto the floor.

"Ow. That was painful. Please, there's no need for fear."

I clicked my pincers reflexively. "What are you?"

"I'm like you, Alti."

Quatra's feminine form was shed in favor of the creature's blockier physique. His complexion was solid and shiny, as though his flesh were made from industrial material. Thick, underpopulated hairs grew from his head like sensory bristles, while much finer quills ran down his arms. At once, I saw that he had pincers just like mine.

He emerged from his brittle cocoon and regarded me in a milky-eyed way, though his features spoke kindness. "My name is Yuan."

"Why do you look like Quatra?"

Yuan pushed the flaking remnants away, which now—admittedly—did not look much like her at all. "I can't control how you perceive me. But you rescued me from something awful. Thank you."

I pushed my aching heart back into my chest. "Were you guarding the tangerine grove?"

"No." He cocked his head, almost bird-like. "Despite how it looks, it isn't in their interest to prevent you from eating the tangerines."

I didn't know what to say to that.

Yuan stood from the floor. "Do you wish to die? That's not a threat. I can see that you're in pain. I want to know your intentions."

"How do you know my name?" I bit the inside of my mouth. "And what's it matter to you?"

"Are you going to kill yourself?"

I thought about never seeing Quatra again and my vision immediately narrowed into a fuzzy tunnel, the panic swelling in my chest.

"Why not?"

"There's someone out there who needs me," I said. "I have to find her."

"Someone." Yuan's tone was affable but he didn't move a single extra muscle.

"Someone who means a lot to me."

"Do you love her?"

My teeth clenched, my composure slipping away. "I don't know."

"You don't know?"

"I don't know if I know what love is." My extremities shook, my eyes searching for something that wasn't there. "I promised I would come for her, that I would fight for her, so that's what I'm going to do. The rest doesn't matter. I can't give up."

"You would do anything? Even though you're uncertain?"

"Yes," I said, the word shaking me to the core. "Because

she is mine and I am hers. I don't even care if I die."

Yuan clicked his pincers, his skin shiny and full of life. "That's exactly what I wanted to hear. You can't give up. Perseverance is the nature of love. And so you have your answer."

Numbness swept over me. I didn't know if that was preferable or not.

"They tell you they need you, and they won't say why, but you believe them." Yuan skewered me with his gaze. "To this extent, you are complicit."

"I need to escape." I felt the lack of conviction in the back of my throat. "I just need to find a way out."

His smile was equal measures sympathy and chastisement. "You have not left the Tower because you're not prepared to leave. Your language was stunted on purpose. What they won't tell you is that you already have everything you need to defy them. Your claws are just the beginning."

"I still don't understand why you care."

"Because you saved me. Because we're alike. No one should have to bear that pain alone." Yuan touched my chest, the lightest of taps. "Love is a great thing, Alti. We must protect it. Inside the Tower, love is stifled. I come from a place far beyond all this. Come with me and I'll show you how to escape."

I looked over his shoulder at the vestibule. "And what if I don't trust you?"

"I have no authority." Yuan gestured to the orchard. "Do as you wish."

I could smell the fruit just out of reach.

"But remember this," Yuan took my chin in a firm and familiar grip, suddenly very close and very stern, "you are spinning a wheel, and it will continue to spin as long as you allow it. The tangerines are an anchor. The more you eat, the more you'll feel the emptiness. Eventually the fruit will not satisfy. And when that happens, you'll gorge yourself to death."

The air grew bitter.

Yuan waited and I took a long time to respond.

Chapter Nine

Yuan led me to the outermost section of the Tower, a narrow gulf between the armor and the superstructure. The ceiling was defined by ribbed buttresses and the floor by catwalks, which spiraled around the Tower at a steady gradient. It echoed with faraway movements and was pervaded by a soft hum. The Oysters could be heard going about their various daily functions. In this rarified layer, there were no jobs and no administrators, just phantom noises.

We began to climb. My legs tired after a while but Yuan showed no signs of stopping. It was not until our second break that I realized he meant to go all the way to the top.

"We're headed for a safe place," he explained. "There's a secret here."

Further conversation was non-existent. My entire being was now housed in the acidic feedback of my calf muscles.

When we reached the Tower's zenith, the stairs ended in a small and tidy balustrade, beyond which there was nothing except blackness. Everything was dirty from disuse. No one had walked here for a very long time.

I sat on the stairs and groaned in relief. "What now?"

"We're here," said Yuan, gesturing at the void.

I looked over my shoulder and then back at him.

"The only way forward is to push against seemingly insurmountable resistance. And the only way to do that is to have faith."

"You must be joking."

He smiled at me. "I'll go first."

He took a running leap and didn't look back. I might have caught him if I had known what he was going to do.

With arms at his side, Yuan jumped the balustrade and disappeared into the darkness, shouting "Whoop!"

I ran to the edge. He was gone.

"If this is a test, I want you to know that I think it's stupid," I called into the void.

Only reverberations answered me.

I grasped the railing and exhaled loudly. There was nowhere else to go. Nothing else I could hope to be doing. There was only this moment.

After a long hesitation, I climbed onto the balustrade and, with arms trailing at my side, threw myself into the emptiness.

My bowels plunged, the weightlessness exhilarating.

I hit something solid and smooth, which I realized was the Tower's superstructure. I went skidding along it on a barely imperceptible groove, like a child on a slide. Though the material provided little friction, my freefall was somewhat controlled.

The catwalk became a blur. I fell at a dizzying gradient, the rush going straight to my groin, causing my eyes to roll back into my head. It was pure bliss. Nothing but pleasure remained as I tumbled down the side of the Tower

Gradually, the contour shallowed and my speed was reduced. There came a dip and suddenly the contour was a tunnel. The wind in my ears turned to an oceanic roar as I was enveloped on all sides. Momentum bled away, the tunnel leveling out until I hit the gap. The drop was unpleasant in its surprise, my teeth knocking painfully together, but whatever I landed on was padding enough.

I laughed. There was blood in my mouth, but I laughed— it was so wonderful to laugh. And when the dizzy euphoria had leaked away, I climbed the nearest tuft of mossy material and looked around.

I was in a room of indeterminate size, which extended in all directions away from the wall that should have been the exterior of the Tower. Gloom shrouded the furthest reaches. The tunnel was suspended above—a perforated pipe that shot out into the darkness. There was an ambient glow in the room, which had no apparent source, save for the vast, unimpeded swaths of gray lichens that grew in lumpy pylons atop every surface.

I prodded the tuft on which I sat.

Yuan stood a few feet away. "Welcome to the real outer layer."

"What is all this?"

"The food base. It grows all around the Tower and releases spores into the living quarters. It's a self-sufficient, self-fertilizing organism that meets every nutritional need in the human body."

I picked up a handful of the stuff. "It doesn't need light?"

"Light would certainly be a benefit, but its own needs are flexible. It can perform chemosynthesis and draw from the waste products in the air. Of course, a fully aquatic environment would be best."

I waited for him to continue, but then realized the implications. The Tower was supposed to be hermetically sealed, but was not. This room should have been filled with water.

"As you can see, the Tower is a fraud. Its armor is rotten and its weapons are nearly depleted. It remains isolated, but for how long is anyone's guess. The world has moved on."

I had so many questions, but all I could think to ask was, "Do the Oysters know?"

"Does it matter? They'll never leave the Tower.

Everything they are is contained in it. That is not your fate. The Tower's entrance is sealed and will remain shut until it receives the right passcode. The code was not programmed in the language of pictograms, however. It was developed from a language of the flesh. I will teach you how to use this language."

Yuan showed me colors.

Like me, his skin held chromatophores, but he had mastery over them in a way I hadn't thought possible. His skin did more than shift from shade to shade—colors appeared and disappeared in undulating patterns that roved across the surface of his body in cascading shockwaves, sometimes competing, sometimes amplifying each other, sometimes mixing into dazzling iridescent landscapes that vanished after the briefest glimpse. He was telling a story, an epic, but the pictograms were vast, the nuances too numerous and heady. I gave myself eyestrain trying to map each pigment.

The story ended and Yuan exhaled.

"That was wonderful," I said after he'd caught his breath.

"It takes every muscle to maintain the effect. You're not just communicating with your skin. Scent glands, rapid movements, subtle vibrations—you may not have noticed all these things, but they were there. This technique will help you grow."

"As a person?"

"Physically." Yuan beamed. "You will become a titan."

"But," I struggled to bite my tongue, "you're so short."

Yuan clapped me on the back. "Humor is good. You'll need that."

In the cavern of food moss, we settled into a new routine. My first attempts at the language were awkward, the strain intense and horribly exhausting.

"Think of it as though you were back up there, doing

your tedious recording. But instead of working through a data pad, you're working through your own flesh."

In time, the act felt intimate and natural. Pictograms were distinct from me, the two of us could never be confused, but the movements of my skin, the colors it produced, were a part of the message. To read the message was to read me. I was not filling a quota, but expressing my perception. My perception was subjective, but my existence was not, and once entwined, the two could not be readily distinguished.

To enforce the certainty of my own existence was intoxicating. It felt like firing a salvo of missiles. It felt like being with Quatra.

Although we spent hours together every day, often sleeping in close proximity, Yuan was mostly silent, never talking about himself. He spent his free time meditating or walking around on "guard duty." He rebuffed all inquiries into his past and said nothing about the state of the outside world.

"Don't worry about me," he would say. "Just keep practicing."

I was not ungrateful to have an ally, but the isolation was starting to affect me—a human difficulty that I had not known since before the monsters.

Eventually, I took Yuan's advice and just concentrated on getting better. There would be time to worry once I had escaped the Tower.

Chapter Ten

We awoke in the last hours of night. Nothing felt real except each other. Every detail was extraordinary. The feel of the bedspread, the specter of moonlight in your window, the air conditioner humming. Only one thing made sense.

I pulled on your nipples and pressed myself to your clit, felt you spill out of your own head. Your hand replaced mine, tugging impatiently. We were joined at every point of contact. And when we crushed together, your fingers on my back and your hair in my eyes, blinding me with its smell, I knew I wouldn't last long.

I didn't have to. You demanded me, squeezed me out, and shuddered your way to climax.

It was our first real night together. In the morning you wept.

Had I hurt you? What had happened? What went wrong?

"Alti," you said, eyes in another realm, "I can't. Please, I just can't."

What was it? What couldn't you do?

"I can't be like this. It was everything I wanted. So I can't feel this way."

You didn't want me? I had made a mistake?

"No!" Said with violence and self-hatred and hope.

No. No, no, no, no, no. It wasn't like that.

You tried to bleed from the stone at your center. You tried to push out everything that didn't have room to fit inside you. All you could manage was the word "please." And you repeated it. Because this was what I needed to know about you.

"I'll have to operate," I said at last. "Would that be alright?"

Fear so bright it outshone your eyes. But you nodded.

"Let me get my scalpel."

I put my finger to your chest and drew a straight line below your collar. I was not a steady hand, but the first incision was clean. Your belly quivered, splayed beneath my other hand. I imagined a small trickle of blood running onto the bed sheet.

I brushed your breasts as my finger made the second incision below them. It went wide and we both gasped. The trickle turned into a stream and I thought I could feel my knees growing wet. I saw little dew drops on your eye lashes.

The third incision, the middle one, was the real test. I slid my finger down your cleavage, hesitating for a while to feel the heat of you, to feel you pulsing. The cuts formed a rough letter "I" that bisected, accented, and underlined your breasts.

I kissed your cheek. "I'm about to open your chest."

"Alti, wait." You grabbed my hand. "I'm afraid."

In your blood were memories. Fear encoded. School years of cruelty, friends long lost, and a love that hardened and sublimated when exposed to air. And that which you hated most: the sad reflection of all those years staring back, never good enough. But this was only the bile. The ichor of your worst god. It spilled from you and I pushed until it turned red.

"Alti, please."

"What do you fear?"

You shriveled like a dead flower. "I'm afraid you'll reach inside and there won't be anything to pull out. There just won't be anything at all."

I caressed you, parting you gently. My hands trailed

along your rib cage and I imagined pulling the incisions apart, holding you open.

"Please. I'm so afraid that I'm hollow. That it's all a lie. Alti."

I reached inside you and begin to pull. You shrieked in anguish, the incoherence of the past recreated. But still you held on and you let me pull it out. You let me gather it up.

"Quatra. Look at this. Look at me."

"I can't. Baby, I can't. I don't want to see it."

"Please. Open your eyes."

You thrashed. You wanted to grab onto darkness and plummet into its velvet lining. But if you were going to vanish, you might as well look. You might as well see the face of your evil.

And then you looked.

Held in my hands, purple and pulsing and fat, was the heaviest of hearts. Not shriveled. Not crooked. Chambers healthy and arteries full.

"Look how big it is. Quatra, darling, there's so much inside it. It's beautiful."

You bawled and I held you until it healed. Just a little, but it was a start. No stitches required.

You asked me to stay.

I told you I would make breakfast in the morning.

Chapter Eleven

True to Yuan's word, I began to change physically. My muscles expanded, my bones elongated and thickened, and my form gradually evolved to accommodate its new bulk. My pincers got larger and stronger, each one now capable of ripping an Oyster in half. My mouth had outgrown the rest of my head. I had no mirror in which to look, but I didn't need one. I knew what I was growing into.

"You're learning quickly," Yuan said to me at the end of a particularly long night. "Soon, our practice sessions will not be enough. You will have to return to the work floor. And when you do, the doctor's creations will be waiting."

My eyes widened as I pictured the many simulacra with Quatra's face.

"You can do this, Alti. You'll have to. It's the only way."

Talking with my oversized mouth was too difficult.

I put it off as long as I was able, delaying the mission by several days, but doing so became even more uncomfortable.

One morning I woke up and Yuan knew.

Now half my size, he led me over the dark and spongy dunes, saying nothing. We walked for hours, the air so full of organics I could feel them sloshing in my lungs. We came to a set of doors and he opened them with a word of flesh. Light flooded our cavern.

"Do everything you must," said Yuan, gesturing into the bright living quarters. "No matter how painful. Move toward the resistance. You can't open the entrance until you find the code. It belongs to one of them. You'll know it when you find it."

I stepped over the threshold, and as I turned to watch him vanish, I caught a glimpse of starlight.

Aside from the awful, glaring florescence of the Tower, the first thing I noticed was that I was now too big for it. I lumbered to the Atrium, stooping beneath the ceiling all the way. The unfettered acreage of the Atrium's floor was grand enough to house every inhabitant in the Tower, whether for gatherings or for acts of indulgence. The ceiling was an impossible distance away, yet magnified by coiled railings that soared upward and inward. The Oysters I encountered ignored me with great purpose.

I had the Tower's attention.

Standing at the center of it all, I stretched my arms and felt myself expand at every angle. My skin shivered and my muscles burned with the pleasant toil. Sight vanished—I had no need of it. There was only the weight of fungal air and my body churning with color and heat. I channeled every aspect of that moment into myself and then back out in a roiling display.

I thought of it like recording. I did not record how the air felt on my skin. I did not record the hour of day or the flavors of anticipation. I did not record how the smells of Oyster bodies were repulsive in their otherness, or that otherness could sometimes be comforting. I did not record the distant shuffle of foot traffic, the food source in my delicate lungs, or the way I hung heavy with new muscles that would not stop growing.

I recorded a memory: the day I woke up trapped in the cellular walls of my own corpse. I knew now that the Tower was not me. There were secrets in its body where there should have been familiarity. If I stared long enough at the distant ceiling, I saw that the Tower was almost malevolent—it was trying to swallow me with its grandeur. It was trying to plant me in the ground and grow me into something it wanted. If the Tower was now my enemy, what did that make me? Had I become Leviathan? My skin asked the question of anyone who would listen.

The Tower was listening and the Tower spoke back.

This is a state of emergency.

The Tower has been breached.

All residents converge on the Atrium.

This is a state of emergency.

The Tower has been breached.

All residents converge on the Atrium.

Attack. Kill. Survive.

Feet clattered, doors opened and slammed shut. The air shifted its weight.

At first non-existent and then painfully, loudly, rapaciously all around, they came thundering down upon me in a single mob. The Oysters were terrified, howling, each one a twisted image of Quatra. Even if I had wanted to run, I couldn't.

They piled on with relentless bloodlust, as if to crush me under sheer numbers.

It was not difficult to pick one up and break her.

But it was difficult not to scream when she screamed.

It was difficult not to cry when she cried.

And when asked if I still loved her, I had to say, "Yes of course," before dropping her devastated torso into the crowd where she would be pulped underfoot.

Jagged new teeth went right through her flesh. They burst with heady flavors I didn't want to know. I cracked into bone and bit through the piteous wails of my woman, now multiplied and dying by the dozen. The maimed would not be satisfied. They keep putting themselves in harm's way, begging for death. Mangled flesh dropped from my craw and from between my pincers, drowning us all in gore. Even with eyes full of blood, I could still see her face and all its expressions of betrayal. They continued to pour from the hallways and collide with me. They were limitless.

But it got easier. I killed them all, and the more I killed, the easier it got.

It must have been hundreds later and I felt only low pangs of nausea when I stepped on one of their precious heads. My rampage had transformed the hall into a landscape of bony mountains that welled with sanguine springs, trailing rivers of viscera. There were no pulsing red lights, only the angry, glaring beacon of my skin.

The cerulean walls started to whirl, mapping colors in explosive splotches that appeared and disappeared with precise timing. What spoke was a creature that had always been a giant. This was the true voice and mind of the Tower. And I recognized it more intimately than Quatra herself.

What if, Alti? What if this is all you really wanted?
I know what I want. I want out.

If there is love then why does it not help you? Why are you alone?
I'm not alone. Someone waits for me.

You have slaughtered what you covet. You have outgrown your own body.
I have slaughtered the illusion. I have outgrown the fear.

You are a broken machine. You manufacture sadness.
I am as I was made. Show me what you manufacture.

I could feel the spores of the food source all around me, seeping, writhing in my blood, and they hurt. The walls pulsed with violent, uproarious colors and images. Panic sounds. Panic smells. The Tower was clenching up, sphincter-like. The Tower pulsed again and I pulsed with it. I answered its burning, brilliant, unflinching colors with my own.

Show me what you manufacture. What do you offer? What power do you have?

I am the Will and the Wrath. Nothing can stand before me.

You offer nothing. You are nothing.

I am you. I am Alti.

You have no name. But I will give you one.

I name you Pride, and I cast you off.

Then everything went dark.

I grew by orders of magnitude, the pain so immense I nearly lost consciousness. The nature of my being changed in an instant.

Ceilings clicked away, panels folded in, and levels collapsed. Walls and doors were absorbed into the superstructure, revealing a simpler, grander design. The food source was everywhere, hanging off every available surface that had not retracted. Vast support structures held the black heavens above, and at the center of this new entity, I stood a giant. A long seam of gray matter split the ceiling, its edges vibrating.

Everything was still for a moment, and then there came a cacophonous creaking, as though the lid of the world were being pried open. All was blinding light. The ceiling parted, the final layer giving way, and I was treated to my first real glimpse of the sky in over a millennia. The Tower had opened.

Now many times my original size, my limbs were agonizingly new and the light of day was more than I could bear. But the air that flooded in was a miracle, a revelation. The scent of rain, the bitter tang of salt, and the force of the wind. The air was not stagnant. It did not drip with decay. It was a cold, rushing, enormous entity that could drive storms and catastrophes. It was beautiful.

As I made my way to the Tower's entrance, I saw a lone, tiny figure atop a suspended platform. It was Yuan.

I looked at him one last time and decided to speak. Words did not emerge from my mouth—colors did. The air wavered as if heated and the whole spectrum appeared in serpentine clouds like dragon's breath.

Yuan extended his pincer into the air and waved back, stoically and sincerely wishing me farewell.

I lumbered to the edge of the opened Tower, trailing colored effervescence, and looked out onto the world.

Chapter Twelve

I thought I'd known the sun too well, having lived unshielded and unblinking for a millennium beneath it. But as I emerged into its radiance, walking on new legs, all those monstrous years were shed like flakes of dead skin. I was left exposed, fragile, and lucid.

What I left behind was not a Tower, or if it was, it bore no resemblance to the monolithic fortress of memory. Its bivalve hull was the color of sludge and razor sharp along the edges, neither fully alive nor inanimate. An architectural biomachine. Its shell was splayed by my exit and had not closed. I saw now that the food base was more than human sustenance—it had composed the Tower's organs and muscles, forming the hinge that kept it sealed against the world. Having ripped itself open, the Tower would soon die.

The world was a rocky, intertidal coastline—nothing but water and low rocks as far as the eye could see. Clouds ran in fat herds across the sky, some of them colliding and growing dark with rain. They were bound for a mountainous horizon that was many kilometers inland. Waves spilled over the shore, soothing in their consistency but ominous in the memories they elicited. The Tower was anchored to the coast by a foundation of pale, rubbery mucosa. I wondered how long the foot would tether the derelict structure before rotting away.

I was free and I didn't know what to do.

My stomach had a few ideas. I was so hungry that everything hurt with its rumbling. The growth spurt had turned my body into a furnace and the flames were demanding. I glanced at the Tower. It was open and filled with meat, but the thought of eating it made me nauseous. Its flesh held bad memories. I just wanted them to vanish.

On the ground, my reptilian feet were devastating, the nails scouring tide pools full of colorful little creatures. Everything looked barren from my height, but the coast was drowning under the weight of life. The Tower's imperious corpse would leave a mountain of carbide and the sea would colonize it. Beyond the waves, a maelstrom of plankton was discernable, pursued by ribbons of schooling fish and their larger predators, but none of it viable.

My jaw was built to murder the neighbors. I would have to find some.

Working with heavy and unfamiliar limbs, I made my way along the surf. I had no skin, only apathetic armor. My feet and legs were scaled, but rest of me was covered in the same chitinous material as the lobster claws that had long ago replaced my hands. My finer senses now relied on a pair of antennae which could discern the movement of the wind, the temperature of the water, and the many chemical traces of living things. I followed a distant scent, hoping that it meant food.

After an hour, the shore dipped down and became smooth, almost glassy. No life could find purchase here. There was nothing except the grinding of the elements against one another. A sudden shift in the wind made my antennae go crazy.

The surf pulled back and the ocean opened up. It rose at an alarming rate, building higher and higher. A wave as tall as a Tower came rampaging toward the shore, the volume of it overwhelming. I ducked into the assault with claws extended. The primal force was a crushing blow to my entire body, but I stayed upright and cut my way through. The water did not blind or choke me. In fact, once the wave had passed, it felt good to have my heavy limbs buoyed up. The ocean was full of rich new chemicals for my antennae to appreciate.

When the flood began to recced, I heard their music.

It was a mournful tune, voices deep and dark as though speaking from unfathomable depths. They emerged without breaking the water. Their bodies were effulgent black pearls, their mysterious locomotion smooth and inexorable. As they got closer, I discerned the mantles of slime that covered them, knobby with projections that luminesced. Each gastropod was half my height but many times heavier for all their armor.

I knew implicitly that these were food animals, come to graze on the tide pools. I knew their meat would be delicious. Unfortunately, I was not the only one.

The interloper approached on eight legs of twisted iron, splashing gracelessly. Its slack maw was full of rusty blades, and under its hideous, shambling gait, the jaw swung to and fro. A great cyclopean eye presided from the epicenter of its body, while tentacles bearing smaller eyeballs wavered from its crown. The interloper came to a halt and regarded me.

Its horrible mouth was not meant for speech. A vicious odor was the mechanism of its language. My antennae crinkled, but I understood its words clearly. We were in dialogue.

I am Harvestman, said the creature, its central eye still fixed on the herd of giant snails.

Chromatic vapor poured from my mouth. I had no title to represent in color, only a story. My name was difficult to translate.

Alti? I have never met an Alti and I do not care for

that name. I have met Lobstrosa. I ate her clutch of eggs after I broke open her tail. I have met Congoran. I ate all his limbs and left him to die. You are too small to fight and too gamey to eat. I will call you Guanoman. You may go now.

Would Harvestman let me eat one of the snails?

No. Harvestman clacked its teeth, all eyes trained on me. **They are my food.**

My stomach was making demands of my body that I wasn't sure I could fulfill.

Harvestman exuded amusement. **Away, Guanoman. Perhaps there will be something left after I am finished.**

I was hardly accustomed to my body—fighting would not be an option. Humiliation churned within me, as I tried to remember that I couldn't find Quatra if I was dead.

Harvestman approached the gastropod cattle and the herd reacted simultaneously, each snail retracting its mantle and shrinking into itself. They were black holes in the surf. He loomed over the polished surface of one snail and affixed it with his glare. His eye emitted a beam of light. In seconds, the shell began to sizzle, the air quivering with intense heat. Steam arose from under the snail and its music grew shrill. Without resistance, Harvestman began to roll the creature around, the beam cutting straight through. When he was finished, the snail lay in two smoking bowls, the wreckage of its body exposed before Harvestman's piercing legs and gnashing jaws. Watching him feast made my stomach jealous.

Finished with the first snail, Harvestman went on to another, several of his eyes keeping a close watch on me. I looked away, revolted by the sight of him. As I did so, I spied yet another giant incoming. It was still a fair distance away, but I could discern the bulbous, crimson mass of its caterpillar body. Grandiose antennae sprouted from its head, their hypnotic patterns like feathery eyeballs. It had one mammoth pincer that dragged in the dirt and numerous, smaller arms that ended in talons.

If Harvestman noticed, he did not seem concerned.

The newcomer kept its distance, observing us. Then, it turned to the side, displaying its full prominence, and arched its back. Somehow I knew what was coming. Harvestman struck first, angling his body with gruesome dexterity and firing a sustained beam that vaporized the surf. Even so, I heard the missiles take flight and I dove for the open ocean.

Chapter Thirteen

My armor was oblivious to the impact of the missiles, but my antennae screamed with the sensation. The ground rippled, the air burned, and the water turned to shards of glass. I was thrown to the seafloor. Corals filled my vision, their stony magenta bodies reduced to beautiful rubble. I could hear the snails, still alive and singing their dirges, even though a fireball had engulfed the beach. My antennae stung from the punishment. I shook off my disorientation and surfaced. Everything was shrouded in steam. I regained the land, feeling glossy and burnt. Fearful of Harvestman, I mustered what stealth my body would allow. His olfactory language hit me hard.

It matters not how you survived, Congoran. I will ensure that nothing remains.

A light beam pierced the vaporous curtain. More beams followed, scatter shot and wild. One of them passed through my side and incinerated the armor without resistance. I felt nothing from the wound, but the knowledge that my armor would not protect against Harvestman's eye was a different story. I had to hope that he wasn't made of sterner stuff.

I found them locked in struggle. Congoran was a coiled abundance of flesh and venomous spines. His grasping arms raked at Harvestman's face, trying to keep the central eye shut, while his pincer grappled to get in and finish the job. Teeth and talons clashed, sometimes severing one another. Harvestman had Congoran pinned, four of his legs impaling the wormy body, while two more were occupied holding the enormous pincer at bay. Harvestman had lost all his extra eyes, the dome of his thorax blackened, his stench potent with rage.

You will be incinerated, Congoran. Not even scavengers will find you.

Harvestman needed only one opening to end the fight.

In the midst of their struggle, Congoran looked at me. He had six little eyes, but it was his antennae—those bright and psychotropic fronds—that spoke to me. We were much alike. I knew I had to help him.

And yet I hesitated.

Harvestman could kill us both at any moment.

And yet I hesitated. It was not enough.

Violence had been easy in the Tower—fear had gnawed me hollow and left me without option. Until Yuan, violence had been the only language available. Out here, though, I was not propelled by that desperation.

What if this was just the violence trying to reinsert itself? What if the violence could strip out my new language and take me right back to the Tower?

"The only thing that can take you back is you," said a voice, erupting in my head. "Your language is strong. You must act."

I saw the inside of the Tower. I saw my cell and its cold little bed, the leering faces of Oysters just outside my door, waiting to rape me anew. I saw the doctor, busy making clones. I saw the army of Quatras, their banshee screams of misery as I stomped out their guts.

"That isn't real. If Harvestman wins, you will not survive."

I can't go back. Don't let me go back. Don't let me hurt her again.

"It's okay to be frightened. It's okay to cause pain

sometimes. The fear does not decide for you. The fear means nothing—your actions are everything."

Yuan? Was that you?

"Yes, Alti. I'm here. Do you wish to die, Alti? Is this where it ends?"

No, Yuan. It can't end here. I won't allow it.

"Good. Nothing can stop you. They are as wheat before the scythe."

I charged Harvestman, swifter than I thought myself capable.

He turned his eye to me just as our bodies met. The collision of limbs, armor to armor, was thunderous. I drove him into the water, rained blows upon his thorax, and clawed at the junctures of his limbs. He chomped on one of my claws. No registration of pain, but now I was trapped and I could not keep him occupied. His lids snapped open, his eye regarding me with baleful grandeur. He was the Abyss, the chasm glowing bright, and prepared to destroy me utterly.

Now you die, Guanoman.

That wasn't my name. I told him who I really was.

Colors rioted from my mouth, not a gentle vapor, but a sigil of energy, language of steel that would not be misconstrued. They gouged out his eye and smashed it apart.

Harvestman howled with wordless pain—his language abandoned. I reached past his screams and mutilated everything I could get my pincers around. With another burst of color, I ripped out his jaw.

Stench and spittle and blood covered me. His legs thrashed uselessly in the water. I felt neither pity nor fear. I used his jawbone. I shredded his flesh with his own teeth. And when Harvestman was still, I tore into him with my jaws, ravenous for every scrap. The taste was drenched with the noxious flavors of his chemical transmissions, but once in my stomach, immediately banished the hunger. I scarfed him down in ever greedier mouthfuls.

It took me awhile to notice the structures hidden within Harvestman's body. There were cavities and capillaries, which looked like rooms and hallways. But far beyond that, I realized that there were miniscule beings hiding in those spaces. They were noticeably human. I looked at the meat dripping off my pincer and saw how it writhed with inhabitants. I had killed some kind of biomechanical siege engine, sensate and autonomous. It was a counterpart to the immobile Towers.

What had I done? What had the world done?

As a Tower, everything had been filtered through the most abstract pieces of information. I could find my enemies and I could kill them, but my communication was limited to other Towers. And I only ever talked with Quatra. Time had lost its potency, its passage dilating until the years went by unnoticed. Each day became the first day—that first long and terrible day, over and over again—until it was the last day. Meanwhile, civilization and its conflicts had progressed without my notice.

Was it Death that arose from the ocean to destroy our cities? Had Leviathan chased us off the Earth? Or had they always been war machines—had new humanity swept away the old?

My ruminations did not prevent me from eating. When I ran out of thorax, I considered breaking open Harvestman's spindly legs. It was not until I felt the paralysis working its way through my body that I remembered Congoran was still behind me.

Was that Yuan chuckling?

Chapter Fourteen

I heard them in the dark. The sounds of their industry brought memories roaring back. Feeding, fighting, fucking, cleaning, absorbing, evolving. The memories told me one thing: I was infested. Had the humans from Harvestman survived my stomach? I thought to purge myself, but when I could feel the parasites worming around in my skull, I knew it was too late for that.

"Hello, Alti. Are you alright?"

The voice was Yuan's, clear and loud, as if speaking right in my ear. Though I was glad to hear his voice again, I felt betrayed.

"Why should you feel betrayed? Have I led you astray?"

I'd heard him laughing. Did he conspire against me?

"You are safe, Alti, although you may find your condition somewhat embarrassing. No one has conspired against you. Congoran was a practical creature, and after seeing you dispatch Harvestman with such brutality, he administered a paralyzing neurotoxin through the gap in your armor. He then ate a couple of snails and went on his way. An amicable parting, considering the world we inhabit."

I demanded to know who or what Yuan truly was. Why was he inside of me? I had tolerated his reticence before, but this was something else.

"Are you asking because you want to know who I am? Or because you want to know if you're insane?"

I wanted to know if I could trust him.

"That depends on how you define 'trust.' It has always

been the root of your sickness."

Sickness?

"You demanded a level of certainty that life could not provide, and like all inflexible things, it caused you to rot. Your brain became gangrenous, eaten up with the monsters of fear. Admittedly, I am also a monster, but where others are parasites or predators, my role is symbiotic. Cure a sick host and it will become a garden in which to thrive. That is how I propagate."

But I still had the fear. If I wasn't careful, I could still see the Tower.

"It will always be with you. As will I. One cannot choose their anguish, but they can choose their reaction. You chose love over fear, and that is courageous. I select my hosts accordingly."

You select the courageous and the sick?

"It takes courage to get well. What does the healthy Oyster know of the world beyond his shell?"

I opened my eyes and immediately knew that things were incorrect. My eyes were filled with gauze and my limbs were stuck to the ground.

"You may have to struggle a little to get out of the cocoon. Congoran's doing."

The heavy silk was resilient, but I eventually snipped a few holes and tore myself free. My antennae rejoiced in the fresh sea air.

"Your armor is repaired. It seems Congoran's silk possessed a healing factor."

So kindness did exist in the wasteland after all.

The waterline had retreated, revealing the scars of our titanic battle. Heavy feet and heavy bodies had reduced the glassy rock to a bed of shards. Hollow snail shells lay splintered, their nacre interiors glittering under the fading sun. There was no sign of Harvestman's corpse.

Yuan knew so much. Did he also know how to find Quatra?

"I only know the things you've told me, Alti. But if your memories are any indicator, I do not believe that Quatra has allowed herself to remain locked away. She is in the wasteland somewhere. I'm certain she's looking for you."

The world was large, but so was I.

"Your words would cover even more ground."

With that in mind, I composed a message.

The thought of writing to Quatra scared me a little, for it had been so long since we communicated, but there was a thrill in that fear. It was like getting to know her all over again. I stood in the water, but looked toward the setting sun as it was dragged beyond the horizon, radiant and engorged. The ebb and flow of the tides put me in a trance.

When I opened my mouth, I spoke a twisting rainbow that spread across the sky.

Dear Quatra,

Hello. It's been a long time since I wrote you. I'm not sure if I'm even doing it right. How are you? Are you alive? Are you free? I'm no longer an Oyster and everything is amazing. Almost. I don't have you and I miss you.

I remember the comfort of your voice, the way it filled me with longing and joy. It was like being in the sun on an autumn day. I remember the way we timed our resting patterns so that we could share our stark Tower dreams.

Sometimes I would dream of ledges in the clouds and sometimes my dreams would be filled with walls and high-tension wires. Dust storms would strike the metal as our daydreams changed color. And you were always there, sharing in the scenery, never doing anything, just sitting with me and watching the world.

I think I stopped being real for a while, Quatra. I tried to hide from my own realness and vulnerability, but that only made things worse. False images of you found me in the dark and they caused me unbearable pain. But things only began to change when I forced myself to move toward that pain instead of away from it. It wasn't easy, and the way forward was never clear, but in my lucid moments, I realized that I have never regretted moving toward pain. It has only ever brought me more clarity, more happiness, and more power.

If you are out there, and you can read this, please don't despair. I'm coming to find you, like I promised. It doesn't matter how painful it gets or how long it takes me, I will do it. I will never stop loving you.

Everything,
Alti

Chapter Fifteen

Yuan was dormant. Apparently even he needed sleep.

I was alone again and night was darker than anything I could remember. Darker than anything I could have imagined. The stars were so numerous they made me dizzy.

I could have fallen off the Earth and disappeared into that sequined blackness.

What if you don't find her?

What if you don't love her?

What if you can't make it?

What if what if what if what if what if what if what if what if what if what if what if?

I let the questions run themselves ragged.

There would be no supplication.

Chapter Sixteen

I sent out my letter as many times a day as I could stand, walking until exhaustion forced me to stop.

There were always dead things to eat. Storms rolled in and claimed many victims, flinging their corpses at the shore—small varieties of plants and animals, none of them large or smart enough to be my enemy.

On sandy beaches, I could just fill my belly with the rotting, muddy mess and expel the grit without difficulty. The nutrition was just enough to keep me standing. I kept hoping for a return of the giant snails.

"Why not go further inland?" Yuan asked. "What makes you think she'll stay close to the water like this?"

Because we both loved the sea. Neither of us wanted to live anywhere else.

One morning, while combing the shoreline for a meager breakfast, something rolled in on the tide. When I went to investigate, the object tunneled below the surf. Alive and therefore edible.

I dug out a shell the size of a hill and was horrified at the squirming, squelching underside. It was a misbegotten hybrid between human and mollusk. Vestigial, underdeveloped hands wiggled at the edges of its protection, while a mammalian face—grey and slimy like wet clay—grimaced at me. It squelched as if to speak, but it had no tongue or esophagus. Feeding tubes opened and flexed where its eye sockets should have been.

"It might have been an experiment," said Yuan. "Or some

kind of ecological failure."

A strange noise came from the shell, like grinding gears, then a tinny voice sounded, looping the same question over and over again.

Are you the one foretold?
Are you the one foretold?
Are you the one foretold?

The hybrid spat water in my face and wriggled it gummy teeth.

I hated the thing so much I almost didn't eat it.

I came upon crystalized deserts and craters big enough to hide in. One crater formed the basin of a lake and in it I saw my reflection for the first time. I was a stocky, lobster-lizard monstrosity. I had a reptilian mouth, the wide jaws full of low, serrated teeth that were metallic. I had scales on my lips and bright orange webbing for cheeks. My beady, black eyes were hooded in chitin. I had no ears, just conspicuous black antennae.

"You're quite handsome for a giant monster," said Yuan.

Little by little, I saw the fullness of the wasteland, its possibilities and horrors.

I saw a giant mantis man with a fully formed head on either end of its body, complete with two sets of claws. I had no choice but to eat the claws, though they were made of pain. After that, I just squeezed its carapace until it vomited out the rest.

I saw river deltas abundant with hardy new life and cliffs that dropped into the ocean. Foothills and floodplains splayed from every orogeny in a tangle of habitats. I took special care not to walk through any of the cloistered forests.

I saw a four-armed Minotaur brandishing relics and snorting corrosive steam. It demanded tribute, so I broke its back and gorged myself for days.

I saw an old city drowning beyond the tideline, its

buildings quietly rotting away into meaner and meaner skeletons. The tallest had lost all but a single corner and was now a colossal weapon. The sea held the sky at knifepoint.

I saw a creature that was all wings and eyes, its body an indecipherable nexus between worlds. It spoke in flashes of vertigo and visions of hell. I had to kill it just to stop vomiting.

I saw active sulfur vents that attracted large, pulpy, medusa-like creatures. They matted over the ground in vast colonies, their membranes filled with gases that caused them to flail and ripple in the wind.

I saw a valley of golden fruit trees, reminiscent of the tangerines. I resisted the urge to stomp them out of existence.

I saw tiny monsters that posed no threat and I let them pass.

I saw the remnants of a mountain. It was a hulking crescent, half-vaporized, and peppered with ruins. One of the ruins was a temple, stinking of reverence and fornication. Its doors were too big for humans, too small for monsters. Shadows moved behind the windows of colored glass, yet no one emerged.

I saw the moon. I saw it wax and wane. And though it was peaceful, I could never shake the feeling that there was something wrong with it, that it wasn't a moon at all, but another monster, a predator hunting for celestial game.

I saw storms of purple electricity that rumbled with distant lullabies.

I killed more monsters than I'd ever killed as a Tower, and I ate them all to survive.

I saw a face that might have been Quatra's face.

I saw that face every night.

And one distant day, I saw a rainbow in the sky, and in its colors, I saw my name.

Dear Alti,

I don't know if I'll ever find you, but I won't stop looking. I have to keep trying. I can only hope that one of these messages will catch your attention. I can only hope they are not too faint, too far, too little, too late. Stay strong. I'm coming for you.

All my love,
Quatra

Chapter Seventeen

She was coming up the coast, of that I had no doubt. All I had to do was run to her.

The shore turned into an isthmus of hills, and hidden behind them was a colony of Towers. They were just like my Tower—unbreakable, cybernetic bivalves, three hundred meters in height. There were four of them crowded together. I kept my distance and watched.

They each extruded a mantle of pearlescent white that shifted in color. Their movements were glacial, gradually digging deeper into earth, reorienting. Nothing else occurred.

"If they had any missiles left, they would have fired by now."

I sent out my letter, as I had done so many times before. Quatra's reply was swift. She was just on the other side of the hills—I could smell her in the air.

Believing they could do me no harm, I sprinted forward, the Towers visibly trembling at my approach. As I passed through the center of their colony, one of them split open in a shower of vitae. What emerged was no abominable animal, nor chimera of legend, but a mechanical humanoid, made from all the technology of the old world. It strode with an elegant gait. It moved as if weightless, unaffected by its own gargantuan proportions.

So much work had gone into crafting its face, such artistry in each detail—the curve of its eyebrows, the subtle jut of its cheekbones. I was amazed by the articulation in its lips as it sneered at me. Had they built a war machine or an effigy?

The automaton planted itself, presenting no weapons. It held its arms steady and waited. My mate was near. I would not be stopped.

I went for the robot's throat, screaming defiance. My claw did not connect, nor did the rest of my body. Precise robotic hands caught my arm and its knee slammed into my thorax. I heard something crack. I flailed wildly in retaliation and gained nothing except another blow that caused my whole chest to crunch.

The robot threw me effortlessly. While I scrambled, it stomped on my back. It kicked my head one way and then the other, pummeling me into the dirt. I wasn't fast enough to hit back, so I concentrated on rolling over. Joints popped and my antennae begged for mercy. I regained my equilibrium, but the robot already had its foot raised, positioned right above my head.

I avoided the worst of it, though its foot sheared through the left side of my face, tearing armor and breaking several teeth. At least I had my opening. I clamped onto the smooth, polished juncture under its torso and squeezed. The material gave, but only a little. The robot could not raise another foot without being thrown off balance, so it dropped on top of me instead.

Under the shadows of the once-mighty Towers, I wrestled old humanity's juggernaut. We landed cheap and ineffective blows. The robot's chassis was showing signs of wear, but it was doing far more damage to me than I to it. Alone, I could not match the strength and efficiency of its machinery.

"Luckily, you aren't alone," said Yuan.

Tentacles ensnared the robot's arms and pulled it off my ruptured chest plate. Denticulated suckers held fast to its lustrous armor. With barely functioning eyes, I saw the most beautiful monster in the world.

She the color of a tranquil sky, her flesh made from translucent gel through which delicate, glowing organs could be discerned. She walked on a skirt of writhing tentacles. Her arms were made of gossamer filaments that hung suspended in the air. Her head contained the only bones in her body— the perfect oval of her skull and a beak of unbreakable black diamond. Her eyes were atomic flares.

She spoke with lazurite electricity that ran the length of her body. Rainbows flashed in the air all around her.

Hello, Alti.

Struggling to free its arms, the robot delivered a back kick to Quatra's torso. She didn't even flinch as her protean substance absorbed the blow. The robot was now trapped with three limbs pulled behind it. Quatra's filament arms snapped into place. Lightning flashed and sparks erupted from every crack in the automaton's armor.

It was almost over. The robot could do nothing. Its circuits were being fried.

Suddenly, the sleek, porcelain visage crumbled away and the robot's final weapon was revealed—a rifled chamber, a single orifice. It filled up with devastating light. Just like Harvestman. The head swung around and I could hear all its mechanisms clicking into place, ready to unleash destruction so complete that not even memories would remain.

I threw every erg I had into putting my claws around its neck.

The nuclear heat melted my antennae.

The snap of its neck came just before the eradicating light of its beam weapon. My eyesight was gone. The air was incinerated. And still I pulled.

The head tore free and I plummeted backward, cratering the ground.

My body was numb. My mind was screaming. Was

Quatra alright?

Quatra? Say something.

I heard nothing. I felt nothing. Even Yuan was quiet.

I panicked in the darkness. I would not go back.

I had to open my eyes.

I had to get up.

I had to protect Quatra. I had to love her. I had to live.

Alti, are you alright?

Her words were electrocution. I could feel her tentacles on me.

I saw only the bleariest forms. Where was I?

Was I in bed?

Was in the Tower?

Was I standing on the shore?

You're right here, Alti. You're with me.

And then I saw her. Right before me, standing over the wreckage of our enemy, I saw her fleshy cheeks and monolithic steel and monstrous perfection. I saw her love.

There was a part of me that wanted to run. There was a part of me that couldn't stand the sight of it. I put my arm around that aching component. I invited its tear-streaked face and hushed it gently to sleep. And when my panic was quiet and my body was warm, I felt what I had always known to be true.

I was here with Quatra. We were together at last, never to be torn apart.

Karl Fischer is a writer and crazy person. He lives with his wife and their dog child. Sometimes he throws himself at the wall and makes an explosion noise. This is his first published work.

The New Bizarro Author Series

2009-2010
Carnageland by D.W. Barbee
Naked Metamorphosis by Eric Mays
Sex Dungeon for Sale by Patrick Wensink
Rotten Little Animals by Kevin Shamel

2010-2011
How to Eat Fried Furries by Nicole Cushing
Muscle Memory by Steve Lowe
Felix and the Sacred Thor by James Steele
Love in the Time of Dinosaurs by Kirsten Alene
Uncle Sam's Carnival of Copulating Inanimals
    by Kirk Jones
The Egg Said Nothing by Caris O'Malley
Bucket of Face by Eric Hendrixson

2011-2012
A Hollow Cube is a Lonely Space by S.D. Foster
Lepers and Mannequins by Eric Beeny
Party Wolves in My Skull by Michael Allen Rose
Seven Seagulls for a Single Nipple
    by Troy Chambers
Gigantic Death Worm by Vince Kramer
The Placenta of Love by Spike Marlowe
Trashland A Go-Go by Constance Ann Fitzgerald
The Crud Masters by Justin Grimbol

2012-2013
Gutmouth by Gabino Iglesias
Janitor of Planet Anilingus
    by Andrew Wayne Adams
House Hunter S.T. Cartledge
Avoiding Mortimer by J.W. Wargo
Her Fingers by Tamara Romero
Kitten by G. Arthur Brown

2013-2014
The Mondo Vixen Massacre by Jamie Grefe
The Cheat Code for God Mode by Andy De Fonseca
Babes in Gangland by Bix Skahill
8-bit Apocalypse by Amanda Billings
Grambo by Dustin Reade
There's No Happy Ending by Tiffany Scandal
The Church of TV as God by Daniel Vlasaty

2014-2015
SuperGhost by Scott Cole
Pax Titanus by Tom Lucas
Deep Blue by Brian Auspice

2015-2016
King Space Void by Anthony Trevino
Rainbows Suck by Madeleine Swann
Arachnophile by Betty Rocksteady
Benjamin by Pedro Proenca
Rock 'n' Roll Head Case by Lee Widener
Slasher Camp for Nerd Dorks by Christoph Paul
Elephant Vice by Chris Meekings
Pixiegate Madoka by Michael Sean Le Sueur
Towers by Karl Fischer